James H. W. Clindinning

Sunset Hours

or, Simple thoughts in verse

James H. W. Clindinning

Sunset Hours
or, Simple thoughts in verse

ISBN/EAN: 9783337848187

Printed in Europe, USA, Canada, Australia, Japan

Cover: Foto ©Andreas Hilbeck / pixelio.de

More available books at **www.hansebooks.com**

SUNSET HOURS.

OH! let us live, so that flower by flower,
  Shutting in turn, may leave
A lingerer still for the sunset hour,
  A charm for the shaded eve.

—Mrs Hemans.

SUNSET HOURS:

OR

SIMPLE THOUGHTS

IN VERSE.

BY

JAMES HENRY WALKER CLINDINNING.

WITH ILLUSTRATIONS.

J. AND R. PARLANE, PAISLEY.
1886.

Sunset Hours.

" The Dove came in to him in the evening—and, lo, in
her mouth was an olive leaf plucked off."

CONTENTS.

ILLUSTRATIONS.

SUNSET BY THE SEA.

THE storm is hush'd; the rolling waves ·
    By adverse winds now lashed no more,
Slow wand'ring to their ancient caves,
    With ripples lave this lonely shore.

On these wild rocks and rugged walls,
  Erst covered with the blinding spray,
How soft the calm of evening falls,
  How rich the lights and shadows play!

Day's glorious orb, descending slow,
  Still lingers in the crimson'd west,
Illumining, with golden glow,
  A pathway o'er the ocean's breast.

And see, all scathless from the storm,
  Yon little barque, the sailor's pride,
With canvas set in graceful form,
  Glides homeward on the flowing tide.

My God, I thank Thee for this hour,
  This lovely sunset by the sea;
It moves my soul with sacred power,
  And fills my glowing thoughts with Thee!

Thy hand omnipotent, alone,
  Could form the grandeurs here displayed:
This golden light comes from Thy throne,
  This blessed calm Thy love has made!

And while I ponder o'er the scene,
  Life's voyage outstretch'd before me lies:
Ah, mine a chequer'd one has been,
  With some bright gleams athwart the skies.

How often, bord'ring on despair,
  My heart has quail'd before the blast;
While faith could hardly breathe a prayer,
  Or hope to reach the port at last.

But still Thine arm was strong to save
  Where'er the danger round me press'd;
Nor could I sink beneath the wave,
  With Thy sure pledge of life possess'd.

And now my evening time has come,
  Its gath'ring shadows round me creep;
And I would gladly be at home
  Ere darkness settles on the deep.

O Saviour, if it be Thy will,
  One favour more on me bestow;
Now bid life's winds and waves be still,
  And lead me home in sunset's glow.

A SONG FOR ADVENT.

O LIST, my soul, the joyful strain
    Which hosts angelic raise;
Hark, how it swells, and swells again,
    In louder notes of praise!

'Tis thus they hail the wondrous birth,
    In David's lowly town,
Of Him whose reign shall bless the earth,
    And man with glory crown.

Ye stars that gem heaven's azure brow
    In midnight's solemn round,
O, shed your brightest lustre now
    Wherever man is found.

For He who form'd your bright array
    To cheer the gloom of night,
Now comes to guide his devious way
    With beams of heavenly light.

Ye waves that roll on ocean's breast
  With loud and sullen roar,
Break gently, as ye glide to rest,
  Along the lonely shore.

For Jesus comes in mercy mild
  To bid earth's tumults cease,
And lay its storms of passion wild
  With everlasting peace.

O earth, in ruin lovely still,
  Let joy pervade your frame,
And every vale and swelling hill
  Breathe odours to His name.

For soon His smile will chase the gloom
  That reigns where sin has trod,
And make the wilderness to bloom
  A paradise of God.

And thou, my soul, prepare a song,
  How couldst thou silent be!
He comes, the Saviour promis'd long,
  With endless life for thee.

THE RIVER.

FLOW on, bright river, softly flow,
    In graceful windings through the dell;
We love to follow where ye go,
    And con what ye may have to tell.

Born as a tiny mountain rill,
    A babbling thing ye rush'd along,
But ever wid'ning, deep'ning still,
    And happy in your own wild song.

Till now, a river on ye glide
　Majestic through this valley fair;
Reflecting on your waveless tide
　The sunshine and the shadows there.

A few miles more 'tis yours to wend
　Along this fertile, pleasant shore;
And then with ocean waves to blend
　Where we may never trace thee more.

'Tis thus with life; in early days
　How shallow, loud, the currents wind:
But riper age and broader ways
　Give peace and volume to the mind.

Then, as life's stream still onward flows
　Beneath a chequer'd, changing sky,
What light and shade, what joys and woes
　Upon its bosom mirror'd lie!

And surely as the rivers roll
　To mix at last with Ocean's wave,
So human life moves to its goal,
　So sinks for ever in the grave.

AN EVENING PRAYER.

THE hour of rest, my God, has come,
    Now gently call the wand'rer home;
Enfold me in Thy covering wings,
And fill my thoughts with heavenly things,
        I beseech Thee.

For all the light and joy of day,
And all Thy mercies by the way,
O teach me, in melodious lays,
To render fitting thanks and praise,
     I beseech Thee.

Absolve my soul from every sin,
Make conscience clean and pure within,
That I in sleep may do Thy will,
And in my dreams behold Thee still,
     I beseech Thee.

Darkness and danger are around,
And help in Thee alone is found;
O guard me through the lonely night
As Thou hast guarded in the light,
     I beseech Thee.

And while securely thus I lie,
New strength, new vigour, Lord, supply;
That when the morn breaks in the skies, .
All fresh and gladsome I may rise,
     I beseech Thee.

C

THE SABBATH.

PEACE spreads her mantle o'er the skies,
 And motionless all cloudland lies;
While hill and vale and wood display
New charms to greet the sacred day.

The insect world, with soften'd hum,
Now seems to feel that rest has come;
While slower glide the streams along,
And sweeter trills the wood-lark's song.

The mill, the forge, the scythe and plough,
From all their works are resting now;
And old and young, once more set free,
In various ways may happy be.

If in the sacred fane they raise
The voice of prayer and psalm of praise,
The Lord will there His servants meet,
And bless them at the mercy seat.

Or if, in contemplative mood,
They seek the rural solitude,
There, in the glade or lonely hill,
His presence will be with them still.

Hail, blessed day! Thou art to me
A sunny spot on life's dark sea;
A little isle around whose shore
The surging billows break no more;

Whose skies all cloudless, all serene,
O'er-arch fair hills of living green,
And healing streams, that still make glad
The poor, the weary, and the sad.

This day is Thine; its hours, its all,
   A heavenly impress bear;
Father, our wand'ring thoughts recall,
   That we its joys may share.

Weary and worn with toil and pain,
   We hail this season blest;
Now love unbinds the six days chain,
   And gives the weary rest.

Calm as the world around us lies
   O may our spirit be;
And cloudless as yon azure skies
   The faith that looks to Thee.

Thy bounteous table, Lord, is spread
   For all who feel their need;
O let us share the children's bread,
   On heavenly manna feed.

Still, as of old, by Elim's palm
    The living water flows;
And still in Gilead there is balm
    For human wants and woes.

O may we drink of these pure rills
    And all their virtues prove;
While Jesus on each soul distils
    His healing balm of love.

And, Lord, above the hills of time,
    From Pisgah's lofty brow;
We fain would scan a brighter clime,
    And see Thy glory now.

Now in the crimson tinted West
The Sabbath sun goes down to rest;
While tuneful birds on every spray
Trill forth a joyous, parting lay;
And nature breathes, from land and sea,
Her grateful incense, Lord, to Thee.
Shall I be silent? Nay, no more;
While all around me thus adore,
I too would praise Thee, Lord of Heaven,
For Sabbath blessings richly given;
And dream, the while, that earth may prove,
Ere long, a land of rest and love,
Where never more sin's blight shall fall,
Nor morn again to labour call.

MARY OF MAGDALA.

'TWAS early morn, the twilight lay
    On Salem's holy hill;
And some few stars with less'ning ray
    Shone o'er Golgotha still:

Where, through the gloom, might be descried
    The Roman cross of shame—
On which "the Man of Sorrows" died,
    Who to redeem us came.

Such was the hour, the scene, when stole
    An outcast to His grave;
A lowly one, whose trembling soul
    Had felt His power to save.

And who, of all His friends, more meet
    To pay sad tribute there,
Than her who wash'd with tears His feet,
    And wiped them with her hair?

Sunset Hours.

Ah, see how pale her graceful brow,
    Her eyes, with weeping sore;
But 'tis not sin that wounds her now,
    For she has sinn'd no more.

The tomb is empty where the Lord
    For two sad days had lain;
Nor knows she yet the blessed word
    That He would rise again.

So, all around that sacred spot
    She looks with anxious eyes;
And weeps because she knoweth not
    Where now her Master lies.

But hush—upon her list'ning ear
    The name of " Mary " falls;
O joy! the Lord Himself is near,
    It is His voice that calls!

How blessed must this morning be,
    Thou lowly Magdalene;
The risen Lord hath talked with thee,
    His face thine eyes have seen.

'Twas thine the latest tear to shed
  When death His sorrows closed;
Thine first to hail Him from the dead,
  With holy joy composed.

Nor, Mary, canst thou all alone
  Such weight of gladness bear;
To others make His rising known,
  That they thy joy may share.

His little flock, oppress'd and sad,
  Some comfort sorely need;
Haste, with these tidings make them glad,
  "The Lord has ris'n indeed."

GETHSEMANE.

THE pascal meal is over now,
 To them a sad, yet blessed one;
And down Moriah's rocky brow
 The lowly Nazarenes have gone.

Ah, whither went their weary feet
 O'er Kidron's vale so dark and still?
Were they with other friends to meet
 In Mary's home on Beth'ny's hill?

Not thither then the Master led
  The little flock He lov'd so well;
Nor to the mountains where He fed
  The weary ones when evening fell.

Gethsem'ne's olive grove once more
  Will throw its shadows round the Lord;
And to His friends, whose hearts are sore,
  A quiet resting-place afford.

And there they linger, sad and worn,
  Their words but few, their thoughts profound:
Till sleep, that friend of all that mourn,
  Low lays them on the fragrant ground.

'Tis midnight now; the glorious moon
  O'er Olivet her splendour shows;
And trials new, alas, too soon,
  Will rudely break their short repose.

O, little flock, enjoy your sleep,
  While undisturbed the moments roll;
Watch with your Lord ye cannot keep,
  Nor share the conflict of His soul.

Alone, beneath the olives' shade,
   "The Man of Sorrows" meekly knelt,
And there in agony He prayed,
   But who may tell the pangs He felt!

No human eye beheld Him there,
   None saw His blood-sweat trickling slow;
And heaven alone could hear His prayer
   That sprang from more than mortal woe.

Ah! wherefore rose that pleading cry,
   Why fell those drops of crimson hue?
Say, did the Sinless fear to die,
   Ere yet the cross had met His view?

The traitor's kiss, in friendly guise,
   The crown of thorns and bitter gall;
His creatures' rage and mocking cries—
   All this might well His soul appal.

But O, to feel, through all His frame,
   The poison of the serpent's breath,
And, nail'd upon the tree of shame,
   To pour His soul out unto Death :—

This was the cup that woke His fears,
  That filled the Sinless with dismay;
And trembling, with strong cries and tears,
  He prayed that it might pass away.

But no! that cup His Father gave,
  Nought else for sinners could atone:
To ransom souls doomed to the grave,
  The Saviour must lay down His own.

The flesh was weak, and might have failed
  The awful ordeal to endure,
Had not Almighty love prevailed
  To make Redemption's purpose sure.

That lonely Man was God's own Son,
  The Lamb to be for sinners slain;
And O, His prayer, "Thy will be done,"
  Revealed the Power that did sustain.

And when He comes, a glorious King,
  The travail of His soul to see,
Creation then with joy shall ring,
  From sin and death for ever free.

Bethlehem.

CHRISTMAS.

O JOYFUL were the notes, and long,
That filled the starry dome,
When angels sang, in wondrous song,
That Christ, the Lord, had come;

Christmas.

And lovely was the morning star
   That o'er Ephrata smiled,
When came the wise men from afar
   To hail the Holy Child.

And while this morn, in gladsome strain,
   We celebrate His birth;
'Tis joy to know that soon again
   The Lord will come to earth.

Not as a "Man of Sorrows" then
   To suffer and to die;
But as the Saviour—King of men,
   With glory from on high.

Then all who in His love abide,
   Asleep, or waking still,
Shall rise immortal, glorified,
   And heavenly places fill.

A PILGRIM'S SONG.

AH me, how long and dreary
　　The "little while" appears!
And, sometimes faint and weary,
　　I yield to doubts and fears.

The road becomes more lonely
　　As friends grow less each day;
For kindred spirits only
　　Can commune by the way.

Dark clouds will often cover
　　The goal to which I tread;
While mists still round me hover,
　　And chilling coldness shed.

Then there are times of sorrow
　　That pilgrims only know;
And burdens for the morrow
　　Will bow the spirit low.

But mix'd with all the sadness,
　The weariness and pain,
There are some drops of gladness,
　Some cordials to sustain.

How sweet Salvation's story,
　What balm in Jesus' love !
And hope of coming glory
　Will lift the soul above !

Ere long with kindred sleeping
　In shades my Saviour blest,
Safe in His gracious keeping,
　This weary one shall rest.

That sleep shall know no waking
　Through dreams of pain or care,
Nor strife, nor tumult breaking,
　Disturb the silence there.

But not, dear Lord, for ever
　Shall this my portion be ;
The grave can only sever
　A little while from thee.

E

Soon through its chambers holy,
  Through all creation round,
To call the meek and lowly,
  The trump of God shall sound.

When, all Thy likeness wearing,
  The quick and dead shall rise,
And, in Thy glory sharing,
  Shall meet Thee in the skies.

Then, farewell Death for ever,
  With all its train of woe;
And, welcome Life that never
  Shall sin or sorrow know.

THE VILLAGE CHURCH.

HOW lovely is the Sabbath morn
    When Autumn days are nigh;
When wave the fields of yellow corn
    Beneath a cloudless sky.

It is the morn, of morns most fair,
  Of earthly boons the best;
The time when we forget our care,
  And stretch our limbs to rest.

How quiet now the village lies,
  How still the village green!
No sounds of mirth or labour rise
  To mar the peaceful scene.

And crowning yonder verdant slope
  The village church appears;
Dear house of prayer, and door of hope,
  Grown gray with lapse of years.

Now softly through its open door
  And panes of ancient hue,
The golden beams of morning pour,
  And gild each oaken pew.

And from the elms that cluster near
  A cooling shadow falls;
While sparrows, without let or fear,
  Chirp in the ivied walls.

Our fathers, by devotion mov'd,
   For God that temple made;
And in its courts, so much belov'd,
   Their solemn vows were paid.

Hard by its walls, with grass o'ergrown,
   Their lowly graves are found;
Some with, and some without, a stone
   To mark the holy ground.

What weary years have come and gone,
   What joys and sorrows fled,
Since they were carried, one by one,
   To rest with kindred dead!

But graceful on its rounded hill
   Their fane still points on high;
A temple for the living still,
   Where they may learn to die.

And still, as holy days come round,
   And all their joys unfold,
Their children in its courts are found,
   As they were found of old.

There rich and poor in common meet
  Where *castes* no more divide;
As brethren round the Mercy Seat,
  They worship side by side.

One spirit fills the pious throng,
  And moulds their simple prayers;
One joy pervades their swelling song,
  One hope of glory theirs.

And while devotion thus employs
  Each willing heart and voice,
They share their fathers' Sabbath joys,
  And in their hopes rejoice.

Lord, may Thy servants ever be
  Thus one in faith and love,
Till raised and glorified by Thee,
  They form Thy church above.

And O, till then, keep open wide
  Our village churches all,
That there, at morn and eventide,
  Men on Thy name may call.

WHERE ARE THE DEAD?

WHERE are the dead; O, where are they
    Who from our midst have pass'd away,
No more with us on earth to bear
Life's burdens, or its sorrows share?
We pause and scan with anxious eye,
The far off depths of yonder sky;
But moon and stars heed not our call;
Unmov'd they shine in silence all,
And cheer the living world below;
But of the dead they nothing know.

Where are the dead? Earth answers, See
How vast the multitude with me,
Form'd of my clay, to clay returned,
Some all unwept, some deeply mourn'd.
On mountain side, in vale, around,
Their graves in every land are found,
So num'rous that the living tread
Unconsciously upon the dead,
And careless turn with spade and plough
Their dust unknown, unhonour'd now.

Where are the dead? The Ocean's roar
Sad sounding on the lonely shore,
Bears to our hearts, in mournful tone,
A message from her depths unknown,
To tell that there, from human ken,
Lie millions of forgotten men,
Enshrouded in primeval gloom;
The sea that wreck'd, that sea their tomb,
While winds and waves their dirges sing,
And wild birds join with answ'ring wing.

Where are the dead? Within their graves,
On hill, in plain, beneath the waves;
There good and bad alike repose,
Congenial friends, relentless foes,
Their virtues, and their vices all,
Before them gone, beyond recall.
And O, what factors these will be,
What items full of destiny,
When Heaven the page of life unrolls,
And seals the fate of human souls!

CHINNERETH.

EMBOSOM'D in its graceful hills,
 The vale of Chinn'reth lies,
A sunny land of brooks and rills,
 O'er-arched with golden skies.

F

But there are sounds of joy no more
 Where joy was wont to be;
And silence marks the lonely shore
 Of Chinn'reth's lonelier sea.

O then let no vain thoughts of mine,
 No things of earth intrude;
The halo of a Life Divine
 Pervades this solitude.

Once in this land the Son of God
 A lowly dwelling found;
These now deserted paths He trod,
 And made them holy ground.

Still sweetly bloom the mountain flowers
 Where Jesus knelt in prayer;
And ever in night's solemn hours
 The stars shine brightest there.

Here, round Him drew at eventide
 The poor, the sick, the sad;
And while His power their needs supplied,
 His mercy made them glad.

Yon lovely sea once felt His tread,
  Once bore His sleeping form;
Its winds and waves before Him fled,
  When He rebuk'd the storm.

And still He speaks from shore and sea,
  From vale and mountain crest :—
"Come, weary sinners, unto Me,
  And I will give you rest."

Amen, dear Lord, our hearts reply;
  Weary, and sad, and poor,
To Thee we lift the suppliant eye,
  And trust Thy promise sure.

O take our guilt and fears away,
  All unbelief remove;
That we, thus blessèd, day by day,
  Thy sacred rest may prove:

Till in a fairer land than this,
  Beneath screner skies,
We share the pure unsullied bliss
  Thy presence, Lord, supplies.

"AND WHEN THE EVENING WAS COME HE
WAS THERE ALONE."

WHERE'ER He journeyed day by day,
    What blessings marked His wondrous way,
Who came eternal life to give :—

The sick He healed, the hungry fed,
In quiet paths the weary led,
And bade the dead arise and live.

And when the busy day was done,
And home the wond'ring crowds had gone,
He sought some calm and silent shade;
And there alone, while others slept,
"The Man of Sorrows" vigil kept,
And for the sad and sinful prayed.

And now, perchance, the mild gazelle
May roam where soft His footsteps fell,
Far from the beaten paths of men:
And Chinn'reth's wave, or mountain rill,
Relieve the solemn silence still,
Where Jesus bow'd in worship then.

But O, Thou blessed Son of God,
I may not tread where Thou hast trod,
Nor kneel where Thou hast knelt in prayer;
'Tis only mine in dreams to trace
Thy lonely path, and holy place,
And fancy what Thy pleadings were.

Nor this alone my fancy tries;
Up to yon heaven she fain would rise,
And see Thee on Thy glorious throne;
The same sure friend of want and woe,
As when Thou liv'dst with men below,
And made their sorrows all Thine own.

And oh, when troubles round me press,
And sad I mourn in loneliness,
How sweet this blessed thought will be!
'Twill cheer my poor desponding heart,
And brighter hopes and joys impart,
To know that Thou still car'st for me

THE ROBIN.

THE pale November sun had set,
  And closed a cheerless day,
When on his perch, still ling'ring yet,
  A Robin sang his lay.

The changeful wind was cold and keen,
  Bleak were the fields, and bare ;
And darkness gath'ring o'er the scene
  Hid all the beauty there.

It matter'd not; that lonely bird
 Of all oblivious seem'd;
Far other things his bosom stirr'd,
 Of brighter days he dream'd.

In genial Spring, and Summer's glow,
 A happy life he led;
Nor less when Autumn soft and low,
 Her russet bounties spread.

And though no barn or store had he
 For Winter time prepared,
He felt some Power he could not see
 Still kindly for him cared.

So for the present and the past,
 For all that Power had given;
His cheery song rose on the blast,
 A tribute sweet to heaven.

And while he sang, could I do less
 Than lift my heart in praise
To that same Power whose kindliness
 Had follow'd all my days?

Thus far through life's revolving years,
  In sunshine and in shade,
For all my wants, so mix'd with fears,
  He had provision made.

Nor can I doubt His goodness now
  When winter time is here,
And like a leafless, bending bough,
  I feel its storms severe.

Nay, rather let me look above,
  And still in Him confide ;
No season ever bounds His love,
  No clouds from Him can hide.

He knows my needs, He knows my frame,
  Regards my feeblest cry ;
And O, His goodness, still the same,
  Will all my wants supply.

SUNSET.

FAST fading from my raptur'd view,
　　In gorgeous clouds of crimson'd hue,
Day's circling orb, with glory crown'd,
　　Again has reach'd his empire's bound :
And ling'ring, ere he sets, a while surveys
The landscape burnish'd with his parting rays.

　　And Eve, sweet maid, so calm, so shy,
　　With noiseless step and pensive eye,
Comes forth on hill and lonely dell
　　To breathe a balmy, soft farewell;
And Westward lifts her veil, that she may share
The glorious vision that surrounds him there.

But fainter now that vision grows,
Nearer the deep'ning shadows close;
A little while—'twill all be o'er,
Yon quiv'ring gleams be seen no more;
And all on which we now so fondly gaze
Will vanish like a dream of other days.

Farewell awhile, thou setting sun,
I, too, another stage have run;
Like thee, through storm and cloud have pass'd,
To reach a peaceful goal at last;
And grateful own His goodness and His power,
Who makes the sunset still the loveliest hour.

And when at last, through His behest,
Life's full-orbed sun goes down to rest,
O, may He then light up the way
With visions of a brighter day;
And make the grave, through His sweet smile alone,
A golden vista to His glorious throne.

NAIN.

NOT far from Tabor's sacred hill
    Fair Nain in sweet seclusion lies;

Its slopes are green and fragrant still.
    And lovely are its evening skies.

Not now on these fair charms we dwell,
    However pleasing they may be ;
Thou hast a far more potent spell.
    O Nain, to draw our thoughts to thee.

The Lord, who for us lived and died,
    Around thee shed His glory mild,
When near thy gate, at eventide,
    He raised the widow's only child.

And still from thee, beloved Nain,
    Float down His words of love and power ;
Sweet words that raise our hopes again
    When low they sink in sorrow's hour.

Through that dear One our dead shall live
    When round "the little while" has run :
'Twas His to take, 'tis His to give,
    And ours to say, "Thy will be done."

A PRAYER.

IF lonely through the world I roam
Without a rest, without a home,
　　　Lord, here Thy way I see:
The world no home her Maker gave,
No resting place but in the grave,
　　　And I would follow Thee.

If toil I must from day to day,
And scanty fare that toil repay,
　　　Be this enough for me:
Thine was a life of labour too,
With sore privations not a few,
　　　And I would follow Thee.

And should I for Thy blessed name
Be call'd to suffer loss and shame,
　　　This will be joy to me:
A crown of thorns once wreath'd the brow
Where endless glory circles now,
　　　And I would follow Thee.

NIGHT.

HOW bright yon starry watchers glow
To cheer the silent world below;

While nature, on her ample breast,
Now lays the weary ones to rest,
And sleep a sweet oblivion throws
O'er all their wants, o'er all their woes !
And where, in cot or lordly hall,
The chast'ping hand of heaven may fall,
There mercy comes with noiseless tread,
And gently smooths the patient's bed,
In slumber drowns the rising sigh,
And wipes the tear from sorrow's eye.
I pause and listen, but no sound
Disturbs the peace that broods around,
No curious eye doth here intrude,
No movement breaks the solitude,
Save where the river, widening o'er,
Plays with the pebbles on the shore ;
Or where some wild bird, prone to roam,
Returning to her moorland home,
Slow cleaves the air with drowsy wing,
A weary and a lonely thing.
And yet, alone I cannot be,
The scene, my God, is full of Thee :
Nor would I strive Thine eye to shun,
My life, my soul's eternal sun,
Since even here 'tis joy, 'tis bliss,

Thy garment's hem in faith to kiss!
I cannot see Thy radiant form,
As Peter saw Thee in the storm;
Nor hear Thy voice that softly stole
Like heavenly music o'er the soul,
When, on Gennes'reth's sacred shore,
Thou bad'st the mourner weep no more:
But earth and heaven, in sweet accord,
Tell of Thy presence, gracious Lord!
The droppings of Thy love suffuse
The balmy air, the pearly dews;
This lonely shade Thy footstep feels,
And every star yon arch reveals,
Displays Thy power, nor less Thy love,
And points to brighter worlds above.
O, that I might on angel wings
Soar upward through yon shining things,
And see, with heaven-illumined eyes,
Wonder on wonder round me rise,
Till, far beyond the farthest gem
That sparkles in night's diadem,
My raptured soul would end her flight
In realms of uncreated light,
And see Thee, glorious Saviour, there,
Creation's Maker and its Heir.

H

But as this may not, cannot be,
Let this, dear Lord, suffice for me,
That still, amid the cares, the strife,
And all the changing scenes of life,
Devoutly I may gaze, as now,
On night's serene, untroubled brow.
And dream, as human minds are prone,
Of other skies, and stars unknown ;
While yon bright orbs with kindly smile
Throw lustre on my " little while."
And when has snapp'd life's brittle thread,
And, all unconscious, with the dead
I take my place ; each twinkling star,
That now looks on me from afar,
Will then unchanging vigil keep,
To guard my long and peaceful sleep,
Till Thou, with trumpet call, shalt come,
To gather all Thy people home.

AN EVENING CLOUD.

THE ruddy sun was sinking low
    Adown his golden way,
When near him, pure as virgin snow,
    A lovely cloudlet lay.

Detach'd, alone, it seemed to me
    An island in the west,
Calm floating on a glorious sea,
    Where angel-feet might rest.

But while I gazed it smaller grew,
   Dissolving in the light,
Till, in a flush of brighter hue,
   It vanish'd from my sight.

Thus would I rest, my Saviour dear,
   When life is nearly done;
Calm as that cloudlet linger'd near
   The slow descending sun.

And as it pass'd, in glorious hues,
   To meet my gaze no more;
So, with Thy light my soul suffuse,
   When life's short day is o'er.

OUR EXEMPLAR.

WHEN Jesus lived with men below,
  His life His love reveal'd :
To Him no human want or woe
  In vain for help appeal'd.

The poor, the sick, the blind, the lame,
  Flock'd round Him day by day;
And O, not one of all that came
  Went unreliev'd away!

Then, if our lips His name confess,
  His life should be our guide;
And we with kindly deeds should bless
  The poor for whom He died.

But if we live for *self* alone,
  Nor care for others take,
The Lord, most surely, will disown
  The pious shams we make.

EVENING.

HOW lovely are the blushing skies
     When morning streaks the breezy hills;
What odours then from Nature rise,
     What harmony the welkin fills!

Then, basking in the golden beams
     With which the sultry noon is crown'd,
How rich the varied landscape seems,
     How full of joy too deep for sound!

Ah, well I love the morning's prime,
     Nor less the noontide's glorious light;
But dearer is the evening time,—
     That lovely link 'tween day and night.

For then the time of rest has come,
     That sets the weary toiler free;
And fills the wand'rer's thoughts with home,
     No matter where that wand'rer be.

When brightly o'er the rural vale
  Its yellow star is ling'ring low,
How soft the airs that then prevail,
  How musical the streamlets flow!

Then old and young alike repose,
  Alike forget their pain and care;
In friendly chat their thoughts disclose,
  And joys domestic fondly share.

How impotent were words to tell
  The thoughts that move the exile's breast,
When, lonely by some flood or fell,
  He sees that star gleam in the west!

Then turns his eye towards the main,
  And in the visions wafted o'er,
He sees his native land again,
  Still lovely round its sunny shore.

And is it not in evening's shade,
  When scarce a sunbeam streaks the sky,
That we sit where our dead are laid,
  And feel that we, like them, must die?

Then on their graves we trembling place
   The flowers our tears have moisten'd through :
Fit emblems of a dying race,
   And of a Resurrection too.

But, better still ; the evening hour
   Was surely for devotion given,
That we might feel, in measur'd power,
   The holy calm and joy of heaven.

O let us then, while still we may,
   Our prayers with its sweet voices blend,
And thus devoutly close the day,
   Foretasting joys that ne'er shall end.